The Plane Trees

The Kissing Fish

MONIQUE LANGE

THE *Plane Trees*

TRANSLATED FROM THE FRENCH BY RICHARD HOWARD

Pantheon BOOKS

NEW YORK

1186127

For JUAN

For FLO

The Plane Trees

Claudia

closed the gallery shutters as she did every evening, but this was not an evening like the rest. It was an evening to itself, a summer evening, the first vacation evening.

The Galerie Villon was the first to close in the Rue Mazarine, but how could she go on working when the sun slanted across the little paintings that also represented suns?

"I keep paintings the way you tend sheep,"

Claudia said, "but I loathe them. They frighten me. Painters talk too much. They can't keep still. All these lines coming together, and suddenly you get them right in the face, like a bundle of agonies."

She put her hands around her eyes like blinders, glanced at her sheep one last time, and ran away to Diego. Her heels echoed on the sidewalk.

Paris was smothering under the chestnut trees. The boulevard smelled of tar and linden, and the city baked. This asphalt Paris stuck to her skin. Still, it only felt good to leave this Paris when you knew you were coming back. The café terraces were full of people, in all colors, sitting among their glasses.

Diego was drinking a cup of coffee in front of the Deux Magots, looking at a map. Claudia watched him for a second before joining him.

"How handsome you are!"

He looked up as Claudia sat down beside him.

"What ocean was ever blue enough to find eyes like yours in it?"

"You're late, Claudia."

"Roger Villon called me. Jeanne's just committed suicide," Claudia answered, watching him carefully.

"How?"

"With gardenal, the cowards' way."

"And then?"

"They pumped her out, of course."

"Ridiculous!"

"That she tried to kill herself or that they pumped her out?" Claudia asked.

"I can't understand how people can kill themselves. It's disgusting."

"Loving you is a little like dying, Diego."

A blonde poured into an orange mohair sweater made them turn their heads.

"And you," Claudia continued, "you're not really a man at all. You're a phony. She tried to kill herself because she thought you were a man."

"You don't know what you're saying."

"Yes, I do. I know just what I'm saying. You make believe. You're attentive. Nothing can drive a woman crazier than a man who listens to her, and yet after a few hours you don't hear a thing. To you, a woman's like a song you've learned by heart too fast. It's not hard to be indifferent. What's hard is to be really interested in other people."

Some Americans stared mildly over their sun-gilded beers at this couple making a scene. The word "kill" had roused them from the torpor of their afternoon.

Claudia was vehement, Diego vague. The girl in orange mohair passed again. Diego's eyes followed her.

"I'm telling you," Claudia went on, "that Jeanne Villon loved you and that maybe four or five times she thought you loved her, or at least were interested in her. For someone who doesn't ask too much, that's something already. You know, when you're a hundred years old, your memory is nothing more than a few dozen images."

Diego looked at her.

"How old are you?"

"Old enough to know things like that. And I knew they'd pump her out, too. That's the way a phony love always ends. Take me—I wouldn't kill myself over you because I'd have to go through with it."

The summer light flooded the sidewalk. The sun glanced off the Sancerre, the seltzer siphons, the pale beer, the Campari. Paris had its July Fourteenth look.

"If you knew how sad I feel."

"Don't feel sad," Diego answered, immersing himself in his map.

"You've already figured out the route?"

"Yes, but I'm not sure where I'll stop. I'd like to get as far as possible by tonight."

"You'll be spending the night at Fontainebleau?"

"No, much farther. Sens or Joigny, I don't know yet."

"Nathalie's expecting you?"

"She's not expecting me. You know she's not. Don't start that, Claudia, please!"

"She might be expecting you. I'm always expecting you."

"And you bore the hell out of me," Diego said.

The sun was reddening the stones now, and the air was soft. The scaffoldings at Germain-des-Prés cut across the sky.

"I'd have liked to go with you," Claudia said.

"I have to go now," Diego said, pretending not to hear.

"I'm thirsty," Claudia answered.

"After all your sermons you should be. What would you like?"

"Coffee."

Diego ordered two coffees.

"Wait just a little longer, please," Claudia murmured.

"It's too late. Don't make things more difficult than they are. It might not all be over between us yet."

"How could it be? Nothing has started."

Diego looked at her, exasperated. "Can't you talk about anything else?"

"It's true," Claudia sighed. "I loved you for two, it should have been possible."

Diego swallowed his coffee quickly, without sugar.

"Let me come with you a little of the way," Claudia pleaded.

"I told you I wanted to drive late tonight."

"That doesn't matter. You can drop me off just outside Paris. I don't want to leave you here. It's unworthy of us."

Diego hesitated a second.

"What will you do after?"

"I'll come back. I have a date. It's so silly leaving each other in Paris."

"All right," Diego said. "But will you be able to get a train back?"

"There are trains every ten minutes all over the world. I'd rather think about you in a train than walking the streets in tears."

"Waiter!"

"Maybe we could have dinner together too."

Diego didn't answer.

"I love you, you know, and that's how I'd like to leave you."

People were buying newspapers at the Saint-Germain-des-Prés kiosk.

"I don't even feel like buying papers any more," Diego said.

"That's because you write them all year long."

"No, it's because I feel I'm on vacation already."

"Your first bachelor vacation?"

"I've never been married, Claudia."

"Love is a wedding; you were married all right. I think you still are."

"Come on, then. Let's get going."

Claudia stood up happily. Diego paid for the coffee and folded up the map. As he left he looked back at the orange girl, who had sat down beside a boy in a checked jacket.

Claudia was beaming. The Porte d'Italie was really the gateway to the sun. Children were galloping away on merry-go-round horses. Claudia watched the shops on the Avenue d'Italie slide past. She abandoned them for a road without windows, without desire. *If he really loved me,* she thought, *if he loved me so he couldn't see*

straight, I wouldn't care if I never had another
sweater the rest of my life.

Everything in the world that distracted her
from Diego went by. Pointed shoes, nylon lace
(recipe: to forget men, buy what attracts them).
She smiled, remembering a pair of shoes she had
seen with Nathalie, a pair of shoes that looked
like champagne glasses. "They're trotters," the
salesgirl said. Nathalie and Claudia had burst
out laughing. And now Nathalie was trotting
along beside someone else on her mauve stalac-
tites. That day Claudia had bought "caravels,"
eucalyptus pumps called caravels.

"You walk like a duck in your caravels,"
Nathalie had said. "Little girl, you'll never be a
lady."

The tremendous blue sign of the highway garage told them they were outside the city. As they
passed the Kremlin-Palace, Claudia shivered at
the sight of a poster.

"That was Nathalie. Did you see?" she asked.

"How does it make you feel, seeing her on posters?"

"I don't feel anything. It's not Nathalie on the posters, it's what people think she is."

"For me it's different," Claudia said. "I began loving her on posters."

"You're always running after idols. If someone's famous, you think he has a secret."

"Listen, people on posters can't help being a little less stupid than the rest."

"I'm not so sure," Diego said. "That Nicholas looks stupid enough to me."

"Maybe, but Nathalie's face is everywhere now, and Nathalie's face is different."

"It's nothing at all," Diego said. "It's not Nathalie, I told you."

"It's not, but it is. That's what being an actress means."

"No," Diego said, "she was an actress when I knew her, when I used to go into her room and find her in tears in front of her mirror, acting *The Seagull*, or Desdemona, or Antigone."

"And now?"

"Now she's a showgirl."

"You don't have to be mean just because you're jealous. It's true she's giving us the slip, but she belongs to us even so. It's just that there are two of her now instead of one."

"There's always been only one Nathalie."

"No woman is ever just one. It takes a man to be monotonous."

At a red light they glanced at a circus poster. THE GREATEST CIRCUS IN THE WORLD, ALL REAL ACTS ALL REAL, the scarlet canvas screamed. Nathalie the lion tamer, Nathalie the tigress.

"When did Nathalie begin to be really famous?" Claudia asked.

"For us, being famous meant we stopped being poor. In one film Nathalie made more than either of us had earned in five years. She said it wasn't fair and gave everybody presents. It was after that that things started to be terrible."

"What do you mean, after that?"

"Because of the movies. When she began coming out on all the posters. When people whispered if they saw us come in, when they started calling me Madame Néry's lover, then it was over."

"I see," Claudia said. "It was your vanity that suffered."

"No, but once you start wincing in front of a flashbulb, you lose your truth. You become other people's truth, or other people's lies, but not yourself any more. It's the movies that spoiled Nathalie."

"How possessive you are. Nathalie's posters always made me proud."

"Because you can't imagine how terrible it is seeing someone you've loved decompose."

"Probably I loved her less than you did. I liked it when people asked for her autograph, I liked being envied because I was with her, I liked her to be recognized."

"But Claudia, I told you she was recognized for something she wasn't."

"She was recognized for what she was, too."

The red lights dangled over their heads on invisible wires. A crane shifted, black against the sky. An automobile graveyard succeeded the usual kind. Traffic was heavy. Diego passed an enormous truck draped in canvas like a woman. The driver's hand hung out the window, looking like a huge hairy flower. Claudia stared at everything passionately. Even the motor sounded sweet to her.

Diego put his arm around her shoulders.

"You're funny."

"Don't tell me I'm different. I can't stand it when you say that. It's silly. It's flattering, and it makes me stupid."

"I didn't. I told you you're funny—stubborn, pig-headed."

"It's just that I can't tear myself away from you. That's all. It's like when you have a toothache. I'd rather stick with my suffering."

Once past Orly she had forgotten Paris. The fountains of Juvisy were going by, and the ponds. They stopped for gas.

In a café across the street there was a television set. Images trailed across the grey screen. Yet it was still daylight. Claudia heard nothing.

All she saw was Diego. Since she had fallen in love with him, she had difficulty being interested in anything else, but since he was interested in everything she seemed less remote from the world than she really was.

The people in the café were watching them. In his blue shirt, Diego looked as if he was on vacation. Claudia was wearing a pink silk blouse and high-heeled shoes.

"We aren't well matched," she said. "It's too bad."

"What do you want? To be the image of happiness?"

The grey images were still flickering across the lighted screen. It was the first summer night. They got back into the car.

"They're like Greeks around that television set."

"I don't know," Diego answered, "I didn't look."

"You never look."

"I'm not much interested in Greeks around a television set," Diego answered.

"You can't always choose your Greeks—not

everyone can go to Greece and choose, like Nathalie."

"Nathalie *is* Greek, Claudia."

"And she has to be Greek into the bargain," Claudia muttered.

"Claudia, stop that. You know perfectly well Nathalie's father was Greek."

"I suppose he was a god?"

"He was a good, simple man who cooked himself a pot of lentils on Monday and ate them all week long."

"And then?"

"He died—not from the lentils. He died of old age."

"Just an old dead Greek, is that all?"

"If that's how you want to think about it."

They passed the Ris-Orangis Eden.

"Was Nathalie sad when he died?"

"Very sad. He had taught her everything."

"Everything?"

"The world, books, solitude, music."

"And her mother?"

"She didn't have any mother. Her mother died when she was a little girl. Her father raised her.

He was a bookseller on the Quais. That's how she read everything."

"You mean she knows everything?"

"She knows a lot."

"And music?"

"She has it in her blood."

"You see, it's always the same. Only Nathalie knows anything."

"Listen, Claudia, I never told you you didn't know anything. And no one is more aware of Nathalie's faults than I am. But what she knows, she knows. And very well."

Claudia stared vaguely at the mills on the Essonne. Suddenly Nathalie's beautiful face, her pale eyes and long hair, her young girl's body flashed before her, violently real.

"How did you meet her—Nathalie?"

"It was because of music. By chance, I happened to be sitting next to her at a concert. They were playing the B minor Mass, and during the Agnus Dei I noticed she was crying."

"Did she wipe away her tears with her braids?"

"Yes," Diego said. "Did she tell you?"

"No, but she always does that. It's one of her things. And after?"

"I spoke to her when we went out. I asked her to have dinner with me. She said she couldn't because she had to work at the theater. I asked her: 'Are you an actress?' She answered: 'And what about you, Monsieur? What is it you do?' 'I am a reporter.' 'On what paper?' *Liberté.* 'Well then, you can come and see my play, that's what it's about.' I went. I saw her act. The play was ridiculous, but after that we were together all the time."

"You made love that same night?"

"That same night."

They were passing the Café des Muses, in Corbeil-Essonnes.

He's amusing me with his Muse, Claudia thought. "She was living alone then?"

"She was just breaking off with an actor."

"Oh yes, I know, Jean Lucas. Your story's pretty ordinary."

The highway was becoming a vacation highway. Girls in turquoise and olive were bicycling between huge bunches of lettuce.

"They all are."

"Probably," Claudia said. "But at least I found a way to love you that was really bold."

"Suppose I didn't like your manners?"

"You don't like anything about me," Claudia sighed, "and I can't get used to all these impossibilities."

"I don't know what you're talking about."

"You should, running after your music."

A boy in a crushed-raspberry shirt was waiting for the night, astride his Vespa.

"What are you thinking about? Your face is so tragic."

"Claudia, don't keep nagging at me all the time, I can't stand it."

"Nagging, who's nagging? If you told me things, if you told me you were going back to Nathalie . . ."

"I'm not going back to her. I don't even know where she is. Why are you always so stupid and so nosy?"

"Everything for the fisherman," Claudia read, *and nothing for me*. "You never should have slept with me, Diego."

"That's right."

Claudia's eyes filled with tears. She always said things to make him contradict her. But it was no use: he always said what she wanted not to hear.

"I know Nathalie's with someone else."

"Instead of telling me about that," Diego said, "you could tell me what you'll do after I'm gone, and you could light me a cigarette."

Claudia took a Gitane, pinched it between her lips without wetting it, careful not to get lipstick on it, then held it out to him.

"Sleep with everyone."

"That's not much of a program. Really, what will you do?"

"Ask everyone coming back from the seashore what you're doing."

"You'll have a passionately interesting life."

"Yes," Claudia answered, "a life of passion."

There was a little Fiat ahead of them. Inside, another couple. Claudia wondered if they loved each other, if they loved France, and if their vacation was over.

"RA, does that mean Ravenna?" she asked.

"Yes, Ravenna."

"Is it beautiful there?"

"It's one of those towns that's so extraordinary you can't believe the sea is so close."

"And the mosaics?"

"They're wonderful. . . . I'll never forget Galla Placidia's tomb, and St. Peter's denial."

"You, you're always happy as long as someone's betraying someone else."

"But the really sublime thing," Diego said, "is the twenty-two virgins of San Apollinare Nuovo."

"I wonder what you see in virgins. There's nothing stupider than a virgin."

"And there are also," Diego continued, "the martyrs in their purity and their white linen, the whole thing green and white and gold—you can't believe it."

"You went with Nathalie?"

"Yes."

"Did she like it?"

"You couldn't help liking it."

"And you went to Rome, too?"

"Yes."

"Is it true that Nathalie danced in the Sistine Chapel?"

"Yes," Diego said, smiling, "it's true."

"She must have looked silly."

"You know, Nathalie was never silly when she was being silly. It was only when she was doing ordinary things that she was silly, sometimes."

"What did people say when they saw her dancing?"

"They thought she was crazy, except for one old lady who took her hand and said, *'Benedetta da Dio.'* "

"What does that mean?"

"The gods have blessed you."

"And what did Nathalie say?"

"She kissed her."

"If you could see the ecstatic look on your face while you're telling me . . ."

"It's something to tell." Diego smiled.

"Obviously," Claudia muttered, "Nathalie's all over the place. In the Sistine Chapel, in

Paris, in Ravenna. I'd like to see Nathalie in a vacant lot."

Diego burst out laughing.

"You must have felt like an idiot when she was dancing."

"It didn't last long, and I couldn't mind anyone dancing in the Sistine Chapel."

"You loved her for things like that?"

"I don't know if I loved her for them or in spite of them."

"I danced in front of something once too. In front of the Lady with the Unicorn in the Cluny Museum."

"That was a good idea," Diego answered. "And what did people say?"

"Nobody was there," Claudia admitted, "except the little lamb in the tapestry."

At the edge of the woods a man sat waiting on a bench, reading a newspaper. A woman driving a blue Panhard with 78 on the license plate stopped beside him.

At least some people come together, Claudia thought.

A nun was pedaling along on a bicycle, zigzagged with white straps like a policeman. Pointed trees, slender as girls, grew on each side of the road.

"You could fit their waists in the fingers of one hand," Claudia said.

Diego passed the blue and white LUSTUCRU noodle truck.

"I'm hungry," Claudia said.

"It's too early. You'll have to wait a while."

"Will we be driving for a long time?"

"Yes."

"It doesn't matter," Claudia said. "Look how the green is fading . . . maybe there's a storm coming."

"Just a summer shower."

"Everything's beautiful in summer, even the rain. Oh, I love summer! And vacations! Oh, Diego, why can't I spend the summer vacation with you? I'm free, you know."

"I know."

"You're the one that's not free. But I could have spent this whole month of July with you."

"I know."

"You know, you know. You're as sure of yourself as a dictator. I could have, that's all, and you don't want to. I get so bored spending the summer with some drip I don't love. The beach, the sand, the salt, the sheets in a brand-new hotel, with a mustachioed Don Juan."

"What Don Juan?"

"The other one."

"What other one?"

"My other lover."

"Oh, then he has a mustache?"

"Yes, he has a mustache. But you're the one I love, Diego. Why drop me this way, before the summer? It's so stupid. Summer's just when we have most opportunities to love each other."

"I haven't dropped you."

"No, but you haven't loved me. It's the same thing. You're going to the sea without me."

"I don't like your way of loving the sea."

"You always think your way of loving is the best."

"You know what happens, Claudia. You bake yourself black and you stink of oil—it's not so appetizing as all that . . ."

Claudia was adding up the numbers on the license plates they passed. "If it makes nine he'll love me." The total never made nine. She looked at the Fontainebleau skyscraper.

We could have lived at the edge of this wood, right next to the sky, she thought.

A silvery Mercedes passed them, heading into the darkness. It looked like a minnow.

Night was falling gently. They drove through woods. From time to time flashes of lightning, like falling stars, announced the storm. Diego stared straight ahead, never looking at Claudia. She never took her eyes off him.

"You have a beautiful profile."

"Can't you look at the landscape?"

"It's almost dark. You can't see anything now."

"Then how can you see me?"

"I'll always see you, even in hell."

"And the landscape?"

"The hell with the landscape. The landscape will last. I can take this road with other people, but your face, your face . . ."

At the Fontainebleau intersection, at the little Marie-Thérèse obelisk, he hesitated a moment and took Route Nationale 6. "We'll have dinner at Sens, if you can hold out till then."

Claudia had nothing more to say. She had taken off her shoes, forgotten Paris and even Nathalie, almost.

At Moret-sur-Loing, the horizon was silhouetted against the sky like the Rue de Rochechouart on the way to the Flea Market. Then they saw their first cows, sprawled white as peonies on the grass. A farmer was standing in his field reading a crumpled newspaper. Birds flew like circumflexes across the sky. The road was amethyst and the sky grey. The yellow CUSENIER truck lumbered slowly ahead of them. Several bent trees had leaves growing all the way to their roots, like fur.

TOTAL ESSENCE. "Me too," Claudia mused, "I'm absolute."

The car was warm, human, shutting them in. The car had become her house. It was a black Aronde she would have recognized anywhere. She knew its number by heart, 7857, and all the possible combinations of that number. One day she had noticed—and it was as if someone had hit her—that there were also two sevens on Nathalie's license. For months, for years, even now, black Arondes made her heart beat faster. Diego's Aronde was the house of dreams, and for once Claudia had gone inside her dreams. At night, on this road to the sun, on this road of night, Claudia couldn't get over her happiness. She pressed herself against him. He no longer saw her. She was a woman. She was his. How beautiful it was, this road they shared.

Diego jammed on the brakes. Five or six cars had stopped. Claudia gasped. A car seemed to be wrapped around a tree. Terrible screams were coming out of the wreckage.

"Stay here."

A man was crying.

"Jean, little Jean, tell me I haven't killed you."

A Déesse had skidded, pulverizing a black Dauphine. The cars had collided on the road to vacation. Two summers hacked to bits, two summers in tatters. A dead woman at the roadside, blood, torn bodies, haggard faces, a man crying.

"That one just died," a man said to Diego. "We had a terrible time getting the others out. They won't live either."

"What can we do?" Diego asked.

"Nothing now. I've just called an ambulance."

Claudia tottered toward him.

"Were many killed?" Diego asked.

"Four already," the man said, turning toward Diego. "Don't stay if your wife is easily upset."

Diego took Claudia's arm.

"Come on."

"No, I want to stay," Claudia said.

"Why? It's hideous and it's no use."

"I want to see."

"You're crazy."

"It's good to learn other people are worse off than yourself."

"First of all, they're not worse off, they're dead; besides, what you just said is disgusting."

The man came over again. He needed to talk to someone.

"We couldn't do much to help, you know. Do you hear them groaning? An old man, a woman, a man, a child—just dying here in the middle of July."

"All the dead are stupid!" Claudia shrieked. "Life is stupid too. It's awful!"

The ambulances were coming. They laid the woman on one stretcher and the man on another. The old man from the other car had stopped crying. His dead son had left him too.

The night was black. That was the first image of the vacation.

"Why was that man shouting: 'Jean, little Jean, tell me I haven't killed you'?"

"Probably because he'd killed his son."

"How really terrible," Claudia said. "You're right. I am disgusting."

They were driving slowly now, not speaking, not touching each other. Silhouetted by the headlights, the trees looked like the bars of an enormous jail. They rattled over a little bridge across the Yonne. All the cars on the road seemed to be following a hearse. A knight in armor was guarding a row of enormous plane trees.

"When did you first realize the world was a terrible place?" Claudia asked, huddling close to Diego as if she were cold.

Diego pressed her against him.

"Quite early. I was twelve. I was walking all alone near the Porte des Lilas, not far from where we lived, and then all of a sudden it came to me, all the vileness of the world, so clearly that I was afraid, and I started to run."

"You started to run, just like that?"

"Yes, like a madman. When I stopped, I was out of breath, but I had understood everything."

"You were twelve?"

"Yes, twelve, thirteen at the most."

LYONS TONNERRE AVALLON, said a blue sign. The trees were still there, and the Yonne, and their anguish.

"What about you?" Diego asked. "When did you find out?"

"It was more diffuse for me," Claudia said. "I kept thinking I had understood it, but women never understand the world until a man has left them."

"What do you mean?"

"Oh, before that we idealize, we make ourselves a model world, a Tristan-and-Isolde world out of cardboard and paste, and nothing can teach us anything before that."

"Are you so sure?"

"Yes, I'm sure. Afterward, we take what we can get, but before that, when you're already running, even as little boys, we girls are still weaving bridal crowns for ourselves and still dreaming of The Man. We're still caught up in words. We think about giving ourselves, when we'll have to take everything. Whether we're for or against, that's all we think about, either giving or selling. You men start running when the agony of the world hits you, and we wait for our periods. It's afterward that it all begins."

The road slid away under enormous fireflies. It was shiny with rain. The trees were leaning over. Both of them were hungry now.

It was nine o'clock. They were approaching Joigny.

"We'll have dinner here," Diego remarked. "I may drive on for a while after. We'll try to find a train."

As they came into the town, to the left of the bridge was a funeral supply store.

"I hope we miss the train," Claudia said.

They went into the hotel.

"It's not too late for dinner?" Diego asked.

"Do you have any rooms left?" Claudia added.

"Yes, of course," the woman answered. "Shall I have the baggage taken up?"

"Later," Diego answered. "Most of all we're very hungry." 1186127

"Perhaps Madame would like to wash her hands?"

"Yes, I would." Claudia smiled, and walked down a little hall with flowered wallpaper.

In the bathroom, the soap smelled of hyacinth. Claudia washed her hands quickly; every minute without Diego was a minute wasted. The smell of hyacinth dazed her. She rubbed her face. Her hands were full of woods. She remembered. It was autumn. She had raped Diego. The leaves rustled under their bodies. In bed, she would have been ashamed of the little drops of blood; but on the dead leaves, herself alive, the pleasure, and Diego's head, absent, present, tense, gentle, Diego's eyes between the sky and the woods, between the dead leaves and the road, the little drops of blood on the dead leaves—nothing frightened her then. Beside that road, on one of the days when most women are chaste, because the two of them were a little drunk, she had possessed Diego.

Claudia rubbed the hyacinth on her face. The flowered walls began turning. She was hungry.

When she went into the dining room, Diego was already drinking his wine. They smiled at each other. He handed her a glass.

"It's good, isn't it? You taught me to drink wine, Diego."

"You were impossible, with your fruit juice all the time."

A duck arrived in a many-colored scaffolding.

"The vegetables are all fresh," the woman said.

"I loathe carrots, I loathe turnips, but I love them with you."

"That's because they're fresh."

"I'm fresh too," Claudia said.

"If you think so."

"When you eat duck," Claudia asked, "do you remember that it was *a* duck?"

"No, but when I'm with you I can't manage to forget it."

"You see," Claudia smiled, "it's a good thing I'm here."

The wine was going to their heads. They were becoming beautiful. Everyone in the room was human now. Claudia made up lives for them.

"You see those English people? The red man is sleeping with the fat woman, and the navy-blue with the blonde."

"At the moment," Diego said, "they're eating their soup."

The cheese arrived on a pale board. Lumps of bitter goat cheese, runny Brie, white Chantilly.

"How hungry you get when you're in love," Claudia said.

"You eat too much."

"I can't help it, I do everything to excess."

Diego was sipping his wine, staring at her.

"It's good to have a last meal together, before we're really unhappy, don't you think?"

"It's never much fun to eat alone," Diego answered.

"Oh," Claudia said, "I don't like doing anything alone. I've never been able to enjoy what they used to call solitary pleasures."

"Really," Diego said.

"Yes, it even used to annoy me. All my girl friends could get circles under their eyes all by themselves, and it was always impossible for me. But any man has an effect on me."

"Any man?" Diego repeated.

"Yes, why are you laughing? You always doubt what I say. You see what you're like? You go on peeling your peach, and you couldn't care less about anything. You don't even see how wonderful it is, that marvelous little rough skin, like a cat's tongue. I adore peach skins."

"What don't you adore?" Diego sighed.

"God, I feel terrible."

"Aren't you going back?" he asked.

The blonde Englishwoman was watching them.

Claudia put her foot on Diego's under the table.

"There won't be any more trains tonight, but I won't touch you; I promise."

They stood up. Diego went out to the car to bring in his things.

In a glass case, she saw perfumed soap—hyacinth, rose, fern—and other toilet articles.

"I've forgotten my toothbrush, Madame. I'd like one of these, and a bar of hyacinth soap."

"Travelers always forget something, so we keep a stock here." The woman smiled. "Leaving Paris, people forget they're traveling toward the sun."

"It's true," Claudia sighed, "we're traveling toward the sun. Do you happen to have any espadrilles, Madame?"

"Oh, yes. What's your size?"

"Six."

"I have two pairs left."

Claudia chose a pair of espadrilles that were red as poppies.

"That's just what I want."

Claudia smelled them. They smelled of fresh rope and summer. They conjured up sand.

She walked upstairs, holding her high-heeled shoes like a pair of fetishes. She was leaving them for love.

In the bedroom, she took off her clothes and looked at herself in the mirror, then she washed her face with the hyacinth soap.

Diego came in.

"Folies-Bergère?"

"No, but I followed you naked. I even had to buy a toothbrush."

Diego began to shave.

"I'm shaving now. We'll be leaving at dawn tomorrow morning."

"That was a good duck," Claudia said.

"Yes, it really was. Because it wasn't a Paris duck."

"A vacation duck. God, I feel good."

There were twin beds. Claudia slipped into the one against the wall. She turned over, as if she were going to sleep. Diego came and lay down beside her.

"Little girl, you were sweet just now, all naked with your toothbrush."

She pressed against him. He turned out the light and gently put his arms around her.

She was always afraid with him. She loved him too much. She couldn't yield herself the way she did with other men, but this night she was drunk, and besides she had wrested this night away from night. She began to caress him. How soft he was, even though he was a man, how adorable he was, and how impossible.

In that little hotel on the way to the sun and the sea, on the road to Nathalie, they forgot themselves a little. Claudia played her last night. She remembered the first time, when Diego had come looking for her.

"I've broken off with Nathalie. I'm free. Do you still want to sleep with me?"

Claudia was about to go live with another man.

"Are you trying to get back at someone, Diego?"

"You told me I could always find you."

They had eaten dinner in a little restaurant and lingered in one bar after the other. Diego was afraid of her. He tried to get away by drinking Calvados. Claudia knew the bars in every street. She knew the records in every bar. Around midnight, she had said:

"All right, are we sleeping together?"

He had answered:

"We know each other too well."

"That's what you came for. It's too late to retreat now."

They had had a difficult night, encumbered with memories. Claudia could have wept, she was so afraid she had disappointed him.

The next morning, in a café on the Place de la République, Diego had looked at her. Some boys were playing the jukebox. It was Saturday and they were excited by the day to come, by everything that was going to happen. Claudia wanted them to know that her Sunday was over, that she had just made love (badly) with the man she had always loved, but nothing showed in her face. Nothing ever shows on faces, not sadness or happiness or pleasure, days or nights: just dark rings—but so often the rings are false. A face almost never expresses what has really happened, and in front of the jukebox the empty, stupid, clumsy boys, who could have gorged themselves on Claudia's night, were scuffing their feet in time to a ridiculous tune that said in Portuguese that love never lasts, and Claudia wanted her passion to show on her face.

"Sometimes," he said to her, "I think I could live with you."

"Is that true?"

"Yes."

"And I could die with you," Claudia said.

"We'll get up early tomorrow morning. There's a train at six."

"Diego!" Claudia shrieked. "Please, Diego. Don't send me away."

"You should have taken the train before."

"Yes, but everything's different now. We love each other now."

"Be reasonable, Claudia. You know perfectly well we can't go away together."

"You don't see how cruel you are."

"I didn't ask you to come with me."

"But what just happened to us is like love. You could read it in a book. It's a true story."

"Maybe it was, before," Diego said, "before you said it."

"But you did love me."

"Let's go to sleep."

Diego kissed Claudia, turned out the light, and went to the other bed. Claudia waited for sleep to come.

How stupid he is, and how greedy; a night beside me wouldn't hurt him.

It was hard to fall asleep. She listened to the sound of the rain, her eyes wide open, and watched him sleep.

He had regained his childhood, not love's little fidget, but flight, escape, childhood. Claudia looked at his wrinkles, all his wrinkles: Nathalie, Nathalie, all those wrinkles were Nathalie. Even making love with Diego, she still saw him with Nathalie. Nathalie had made Diego's wrinkles. So much love. So much love. There was no room for her. The faucet made a little machine-gun noise: tac-tac-tac-tac. Claudia looked at Diego.

She remembered the first time she had dragged him out of Paris. They had slept at Vernon, in a hotel with pale-blue shutters. They hadn't noticed the blue until morning. They had drunk coffee, eaten lunch on the banks of a river that smelled of grease. They were happy. Then she had begged him to drive to the sea. At Fécamp a warm light bathed the town. Diego ran across the beach like a child. The smell of seaweed was intoxicating. The tide made them dizzy. The stones were hot. Diego threw them into the sea. He seemed to have forgotten himself. They were alone on the beach, Claudia in desire and Diego in childhood. She was walking barefoot at the water's edge to attract his attention, then she saw him lying asleep on the hot stones. He always escaped. He forgot everything, he had forgotten her, and the smell of the sea hovered over their bodies as he slept. Claudia picked up a pebble and put it in her pocket. She knew there could be no real love between them. Nathalie was there, stronger than death, stronger than absence, stronger than memory. Claudia wished she had been brave enough to suggest a *ménage à trois,* but she was too young, too much of a coward, too fragile to think of sharing.

The trucks rolled through the night like old snails and tormented Claudia. Diego was sleeping like a child. Claudia went over and lay down beside him.

It was just daylight, and she woke up first:

"Wake up, it's time. We have to go."

He crushed himself against her like a child trying to stay inside his sleep. She was awake, wide awake and lucid now, but even feeling him against her was distracting. The world she saw through the window was grey, sad.

"It's daylight, we're leaving."

She looked at the wallpaper. Grey with huge mauve hydrangeas. The hydrangeas were nailed in her memory. They made love in the mist of the morning. What Claudia won from the night Diego won from sleep.

They dressed quickly, like a husband and wife who are used to each other. It was raining, a fine, gentle rain. Claudia had stolen one of Diego's shirts.

"You look nice that way."

"You know," Claudia said, "last night I really felt as if I were your wife. I forgot Nathalie for several hours."

"So did I," Diego said.

"This life *à trois* is difficult."

"It's not easy."

"I never cheated," Claudia said, "because I loved Nathalie, but I was happy when you told me you were through with her."

"Women are bitches," Diego said.

"I don't think so. But you were so involved with her. If you hadn't been unhappy, sometimes . . ."

Diego caressed her cheek as if she were a child.

"You know, Nathalie could do everything for me: make love, cook, drive fast, act. Everything she touched became beautiful. I don't know how to do anything. I can't even pick a flower. She told me that one day, and she laughed. Not even pick a flower."

They were driving through grey mist that made it hard to see. As if they were separated from the world by an enormous spiderweb.

"Which do you like best, mornings-after-the-night-before, or morning-mornings?" Claudia asked.

"I think mornings-after-the-night-before."

"I like morning-mornings in Paris, when the sun's already up and there's a breeze, and green trees. Did you ever notice that trees look like people when there are no people around?"

"No," Diego said.

"And that they're scary?"

"You're scared of everything."

"That must be what loving is. Dying of fright. But I really love trees. What's your favorite tree?"

"I never thought of it. Those, maybe."

They were driving through some young birches.

"I knew it. It's because they look like Nathalie."

"And what's yours?"

"Plane trees, of course. The plane trees of the South."

"A real plane tree is very beautiful," Diego admitted.

"It's more than beautiful, it's tremendous and full of the South, with its bark peeling off, like you. For me, plane trees are summer, plane trees are love and not growing old."

The cobwebs in the grass glittered with dew.

"I feel like coffee," Claudia said, looking at the bottles of milk standing in front of the doors.

"It's too early, nothing's open."

"I want it so badly."

"Wait a little, we'll stop at the first place on the road that's open."

The road was monotonous, shiny in the grey mist. The headlights were like two weak little suns. It was six in the morning.

"You should have taken the train," Diego said.

Claudia didn't answer. She felt caught up in a rhythm of wretchedness. Suddenly she no longer wanted to fight.

"You should have taken the train," Diego repeated.

"You should marry me," she answered.

Suddenly they saw a roadside café.

"Look, there's a light on!" Claudia exclaimed.

Red and yellow trucks were scattered like children's toys along the roadside. From a distance it looked like a dream.

Diego slipped between two trucks. Though Claudia detested trucks when she had to pass them on the road, they were so touching here, in repose: innocent, enormous, docile.

They went into the café. The waitress seemed still asleep. They sat down in a corner.

"Two coffees, one light, please, Madame!" Claudia shouted.

"If you knew how I hate people to order for me."

"After all, Diego, I know you want a light coffee."

"Maybe that's what you know, but I happen to want it black."

"I know you only like light coffee in the morning."

"You may know what I like, but you don't know what I want."

"All I want is you. Always."

"One light and two black!" Diego shouted.

"Even at dawn you need to feel free of me?"

"Especially at dawn."

The truck drivers were drinking wine, eating sausages and bread.

"How can they be drinking so early?" Claudia asked.

"Their daytime comes at night. They've been driving all night long. They've eaten the stars and now they're thirsty."

The men were looking at Claudia. One of them, very tall and tanned, was caressing the waitress.

"You see," Claudia said, "people can desire each other even in the morning."

"I just told you their morning's at night."

"We should be able to desire any time," Claudia sighed.

The waitress brought the coffee. It wasn't very good.

"We'll try again farther on?"

"Maybe," Diego said.

One of the drivers looked at the waitress. She turned off the machine that was making the bad coffee, and they went upstairs. The night was starting over again in the morning.

Diego paid and they left.

"Let me drive for a while," Claudia asked.

"You drive so badly."

"Just a little while."

The road was clear, straight, easy. Claudia sat behind the wheel. She moved the seat forward.

"I always forget how short you are."

"You spend your life forgetting me."

She drove carefully, her jaws clamped, her eyes fixed straight ahead.

"You look like a good girl when you drive."

"I like driving," Claudia said, "and besides, I get so scared that it keeps me from thinking."

There was a big Esso truck in front of them. The road was empty.

"Pass him," Diego suggested.

"Are you sure nothing's coming?"

"Look, the road is straight. You can see all the way to Auxerre. You don't see anything coming, do you?"

"No."

"Then pass, or I'll take the wheel again."

Claudia clenched her teeth a little tighter and passed the red truck.

"You're really afraid of everything," Diego said.

"Moral courage is the only kind I have."

A car was coming toward them down the empty road. Claudia grew tense.

"You're scared of all the cars coming in the other direction?"

"Yes, what if their steering wheel broke?"

Diego burst out laughing.

"If you think of that every time, it's brave of you to drive at all."

"If I talk I forget how scared I am."

A sign announced: HENRI MAIRE VIN FOU.
"I'm crazy too," she thought.

France slid by sadly. The sun rose over its misery. Claudia felt everything escaping her.

"Let me drive," Diego said. "We'll never get there."

"I'm in no hurry," Claudia said.

"I am."

"If only you could look into the future," she sighed, "you'd know that at this moment you belong to me."

Some white hens were fluttering in the corner of a garden, and four old women in black were sitting on a bench near a fountain.

"Stop here," Diego said. "We'll get some music if you want."

Claudia parked at the roadside. Diego got back behind the wheel. She turned on the radio.

A deafening burst of jazz began to dissect the morning.

"I love you, Diego."

"You think you love me."

"No, I love you. I have for a long, long time."

A purple episcopal Déesse passed them.

I love a curé, Claudia thought.

"You wouldn't talk so much if you really loved me."

"I didn't want to love you," Claudia said. "I'm losing my looks and my mind. I never wanted to love you. I did everything I could not to love you, and one night it fell on me like a thunderbolt. Before, I didn't see you, I was free, I was happy. Well, maybe not happy, but I was living quietly with my little problems."

"What night?" Diego asked.

"One night that didn't seem any different from the rest, in a café near Vincennes. Nathalie was there and the Villons. Some boys were playing the pinball machine. I knew Jeanne Villon was in love with you. Nathalie was talking theater with Jeanne. You were listening to them with a vague, lonely expression. You were drinking a glass of wine and you looked sad. I realized at that moment: I love him. I've never loved anyone else, and I told myself—it was twenty-five after twelve—'If he looks at me before twelve-thirty, he'll love me.' And you looked at me."

"I didn't see you," Diego said.

"That doesn't matter. I saw you, my eyes met yours. You smiled at me, and you looked as if you understood me completely."

"There was nothing to understand."

"For months, because of that look, I didn't feel alone again, ever, anywhere."

"It's like a Spanish inn," Diego sighed. "Everyone brings his own dinner."

Some workmen were strung out along the road, pneumatic drills roaring.

What a sad story, Claudia thought. *He'll never love me. How can I find one word, the one gesture, the one memory that will make him love me?*

Diego stopped behind a truck. Claudia read: WAREHOUSE, *Romans, Drôme.*

"Another time, remember? when Nathalie was on tour, I came one evening. You put on a record and we kissed each other on the couch. It was the first time we kissed. Then I was ashamed of myself. I closed my eyes to kiss you, and when I opened them again I saw I was in Nathalie's house. I was ashamed and then I was afraid. I had come because I knew that she wasn't there, but she was there all the same. That was the day I realized I would never be your mistress."

"You were wrong."

"No, I'm not your mistress. Nathalie's your wife, your mistress, everything. I'm an extra. I'm someone who's here."

"You can say that again."

MASSES AT VERMENTON, Claudia read. *Pray for him to love me.*

Suddenly the horizon fell open and she saw the world as from a balcony. Acollay pottery was strewn along the roadside. Huge porcelain flowers sprang out of the earth.

What a funny idea, Claudia thought. *As if anyone could want a plate at seventy miles an hour.*

Acollay was the Montélimar of ceramics; in Acollay you wanted aluminum pans, the way you wanted pimento at Montélimar.

"No, I'm not your mistress. I love Nathalie too much. I keep seeing her eyes, and the idea of not being able to bear having her look at me drives me crazy. It's her eyes that spoil everything. So blue. Maybe I could have fooled a woman with black eyes, but not Nathalie. Even though she rarely looked at me. She forgot about me. She was like you that way. But I could never have turned away my eyes when she was looking at me."

"When you come down to it," Claudia continued, "it's the eyes that do it."

"Everything does it."

"Luckily you almost never look at me."

"We'd be in the ditch if I looked at you."

"No, I'm talking about life. You don't even know what color my eyes are."

"Yes, I do," Diego said, "they're green."

"Wrong, they're yellow. I have yellow eyes."

"Your eyes are changeable, but they're not yellow."

"And you belong to Nathalie forever."

Nathalie's beautiful eyes struck Claudia to the heart.

"It's true, Nathalie's eyes could make you believe in God."

"Sometimes," Diego conceded, "I like the way you have of loving her."

"You see, you never use the word 'love' except about her."

"You never talk about anything else, Claudia."

"And you're crazy about her. It's terrible."

Diego and Claudia were driving between two rivers. *Water's the opposite of a mirror*, Claudia thought. They were leaving Vézelay.

Unhappiness fell on them again. Nathalie and Vézelay. Claudia imagined it all too well. The rails alongside the road reminded her of the ride back. She was going down a hill she would have to climb back up. Just looking at it made her dizzy.

The radio broadcast the news to increase Claudia's misery, the misery of the world. She stared at signs, vainly seeking a solution. She turned off the radio.

"Leave it on, that's the news."

"There can't be any news since you don't love me."

1949 INHABITANTS

640 READERS OF *Match,* announced a village sign.

"There's a market, Diego! Stop, please stop! I have a thing about markets."

"Markets, too," Diego sighed. He stopped the car.

"All my fruit is ripe!" a fat man was yelling.

It was a real village market. The houses were scattered on each side of the street, and the huge trucks were parked around a tiny red brick church. Old women in black were selling cheese, eggs, and little boxes full of raspberries. The raw wood trestles groaned under the eggplants and tomatoes. Long gladioli, like snakes with a thousand heads, coiled out of buckets of cold water among artichokes and lettuces.

Everything, Claudia thought, *too much, even. There are more cherries on that stand than there is love in me.* She remembered all the markets she adored, the markets of the South, the Aligre market, the Alma market.

"Do you have some very light blue-jeans?" Diego was asking a little peddler in brown corduroy.

"You're a real whore," Claudia said. "If you think you're going to get Nathalie all excited with a pair of tight blue-jeans, you're making a big mistake."

"Let me alone," Diego said, "it's your market, not mine."

Claudia headed for the cherries and peaches.

She listened lovingly to the sound of hands under the fruit and the pans of the huge scales. When she came back she had her arms full of cherries and was seventeen years old.

They started again, and the car began to smell of fruit and sunshine.

"Those blue-jeans look nice on you," Claudia said.

"They're not bad," Diego answered.

She kissed him, and spat a cherry pit into his mouth.

"You bitch, you always try something when I'm not expecting it."

"It's a good thing Nathalie didn't invent everything," Claudia said.

Diego snatched some cherries out of her hand.

"They're too sweet, these cherries of yours."

"It's always too something for you," Claudia said.

A farmer was walking slowly toward them beside a beige horse that made them smile.

An old woman all in black, the black of village
virtue, was walking behind him, taking tiny
steps; white stockings showed under her skirt.

"Did you see the white stockings, and the
beige of the horse?" Claudia asked.

"Yes, I saw," Diego answered.

Diego began driving very fast. Claudia was
eating cherries and spitting the pits out the window. It was the road to Nathalie that she was
strewing with little stones, scattering her pebbles
along the road of their love. When would he
throw her out? At Lyons? Before Lyons? At
Mâcon? Maybe. It was so stupid to be driving toward the sea without going to the sea. Nathalie
was probably laughing with someone else. She
knew he was coming. Of course she knew. How
sad he looked. Diego. Diego. Why did he never
listen to her? She would always be an extra per-

son in his life. Was it her fault, or theirs? Yet last night she had pleased him. She was nothing to him. Nothing. Nothing.

She lit him a cigarette, which he took without a word.

"That's the Château de La Rochepot," Diego said.

"I couldn't care less about the Château de La Rochepot," Claudia answered.

"Neither could I, but I showed it to you to be nice."

"What would be nice would be if you took me to the sea, not showed me châteaux."

"I can't take you to the sea," Diego said.

"I'm beginning to find that out," Claudia said. "But if you were less mysterious I'd be able to know what's on your mind. It's your cowardice that disgusts me."

"You don't know what you're talking about."

"You're afraid to say: 'I love Nathalie, I'm crazy about her.' You're afraid to tell me that, out of pure cowardice. You spend your whole life not saying things. I think you should say everything. I can say: "Diego loves Nathalie," and not die of it. But those little expressionless masks of yours, all those secrets and mysteries—that disgusts me. The sea never overflowed because somebody said 'I love you.' I'm sick of all these meaningful glances; what I like is words, songs, everything that mentions love. The earth, the sky, the leaves are here to remind us that nothing lasts. So why not say: 'I love Nathalie,' when you don't love me?"

"It's not because I love Nathalie that I don't love you. There's no connection."

"That's right," Claudia said. "It's even possible that not loving Nathalie you can't love me. I understand you. But I know you *do* love Nathalie, and I'm not afraid to tell you so. I played a losing game but I loved you too much. I had to try. You're the only one who could make me sick of you."

A little red barrier came down across the road. The level crossing was closed.

The train went by very fast. A fat lady came

out behind the three dahlias planted around her little house and raised the barrier.

"What a life, can you imagine?" Claudia said. "All that worry and responsibility for such a little house. She can never make love in peace, poor woman, with that bell bothering her all the time."

"Still, she must manage to from time to time," Diego said, looking at the garden. "She has a lot more children than dahlias."

After the dahlias, the vines. With the vines, the poplars.

"I'm thirsty," Diego said. "It's because of your cherries. Find a town with a wine in its name where we can drink something and eat a sandwich. I don't want to stop again before Lyons."

"Lyons? Why Lyons?" Claudia asked.

"It'll be easiest to find a train at Lyons."

Claudia said nothing. She began examining the map carefully. Juliénas, Santenay, Chénas.

She had to catch his memory with a beautiful wine.

"Chassagne-Montrachet. Is that good enough for us?"

"It's a good wine," Diego answered.

They went into a little café.

"Two glasses of wine, Madame, and two ham sandwiches, please."

In the café ten little records were spread out in a fan like the petals of a black daisy. Claudia stood up, decided on one.

"Listen," she said to Diego. "It's the most beautiful love song in the world."

"It's a pretty tune."

"It's a love song. You should play records more often. It's good for people who are too bashful."

"Claudia, stop that."

"After all, if we drink wine, if we listen to love songs, we can at least touch each other."

"There's no need to touch each other."

"There is for me."

"You think no one exists unless you can touch him."

"That's right," Claudia answered, delighted. "I'm like the Apostle Thomas."

"You're unbearable, most of all," he answered, pulling away.

"Why do you always resist?"

"Because I don't like being raped."

"Oh yes, you do," Claudia said, "you adore it."

"Come on," Diego said, "let's get back in the car. You're wearing me out. We have to leave."

"For Nathalie?"

"For Tournus. A beautiful town. One of the most beautiful towns I know."

"You're the one who's beautiful, not towns."

In Sennecey-le-Grand, a child in a black apron crossed the road with a loaf of bread under each arm, both bigger than he was.

"I love you, Diego."

"Leave me alone."

The world was becoming unreal. The milestones looked like lumps of nougat imitating milestones.

"Kiss me."

"Are you drunk?"

"No, but you're so attractive. You're so handsome, you're not stupid, you're sad, you're lonely, and you have the softest neck in the world."

"I still don't know what it is you like about me."

"Stop wondering. Please. Kiss me."

Diego stopped the car at the edge of a field. He began kissing her.

"You know," he said, "I could have loved you."

"You could have, but you can't."

He pressed her hard against him.

"Come on," she said.

Kissing in the car, in the middle of the morning, their adolescence came back to them.

"Come on," Claudia repeated.

"Someone will see us."

"You can always make love in a field, and besides nobody is around."

Claudia put her panties back on.

"They're pretty, aren't they, with all that lace?"

Diego was still lying under the branches.

"Once I forgot them on the mantelpiece. When I remembered I had one of those hysterical laughing fits."

Diego was still in the branches.

"Diego, you love women too much; it's going to wreck you."

"Shut up," he suggested, kissing her.

"How well you kiss. It's as if you were drinking. Did you ever swallow someone?"

"No," Diego said, "I would have noticed."

"You're so absent-minded you've probably swallowed several overexcited women. Kiss me again."

Diego held her close. "Stay like that. Shut up. Look at the sky."

The sky was grey between the leaves. Some red cows were scattered in the field behind the barbed wire, their calves with them.

"I'd like to have a child by you," Claudia said.

"Come on," Diego said, "we have to go."

Claudia's cheeks were very red now. Diego passed a yellow truck that was called L'INTRÉ-PIDE.

"Women are brave, don't you think?" she asked Diego.

"Women are crazy."

"You don't see how brave I am with you. But I know everything's impossible. First of all on account of Nathalie, then on account of you, then on account of me."

"You know things nobody else knows," Diego said.

"Yes. Look at the two of us. I'm the one who asked you if we were going to sleep together. And I'm the one who asked you to let me come with you now. I almost brought along my toothbrush, but I didn't: out of superstition."

"Superstition?"

"I was afraid it might not work."

"Women think too much."

"No, we don't think at all, but that's all we think about."

They were driving slowly. Like puppies, the cars that passed them showed their muzzles.

"In our case, then," Diego asked, "you're the initiator?"

"Yes, but that doesn't keep me from suffering more than you."

"You don't know what you're saying."

"Yes, I do. Even so, I'm everywhere in you. In Nathalie and in you, but I'm not in your thoughts."

"I'm not in your thoughts either," Diego said.

"So we can never meet."

"Why should we meet? What's beautiful is when two solitudes confront each other."

"But I'm not solitary," Claudia shrieked, "I'm public!"

"Little girl, you're overexcited, that's what you are."

"I wish the days were nights and the nights days."

"What difference would that make?"

"I wouldn't see my unhappiness any more."

"You're a sentimentalist."

"No I'm not, I'm sad."

"I'm sad too, everyone's sad. Why talk about it?"

Two trucks passed carrying tree trunks that looked like enormous corpses.

"Because I'm going to leave you soon, tear myself away from you, because it's our last trip."

"Do you remember the day when we met at Moulins? I took the train to come back to Paris with you. You had already gone to the sea, I don't remember why. I waited for you, sitting there in front of a bridge, frozen, and the earth trembled under my feet every time I saw a light. You didn't come until midnight. I was sick waiting for you. I loved that trip because no one in the world knew where we were, not even Nathalie."

"We didn't deceive her when we were at Moulins."

"We've never deceived her, but I can't help it. I can't help thinking about her. And I can never have you for my own."

"But no one ever has anybody, Claudia."

"I know it. You don't even have me. I sleep with you, I am *with* you, but I'm never yours."

"Of course. So?"

"So I don't understand. I love you in the wine, in the road, in the stones, in misery. I love you everywhere except in love. I'm afraid of you in love."

"Why?"

"I don't know, but you're worse—you're ashamed of me."

"Ashamed of you?"

"You don't like us to be seen together."

"You know how much I like secrets."

"You don't like secrets, you like lies. You're not mysterious, you're a coward."

"Have it your way. Besides, as long as you're going to talk about her all the time, have you ever seen me—even once in five years—with an expression of desire for her?"

"That's what I have against you, now that I know how much you love her. You're a Pharisee, a hypocrite."

"No, I'm not. It's just that I don't think night should overflow into day."

"You're as hypocritical as the bourgeois who hide in furnished rooms or who only desire each other with an orchestra playing in the background."

"I don't see the connection."

"You're ashamed of your nights."

"After all, Claudia, you can forget the night sometimes, you can distract yourself."

"Yes, you have your distractions, your heartless books, your dried-up ideas, your unsuccessful revolutions. You treat ideas like women.

They seduce you and you abandon them. Your relations with ideas are sordid, pathetic."

"Do you think Socrates thought of nothing but love?" Diego asked, laughing.

"Maybe not Socrates, but Rembrandt all the time. Mozart too, that's probably why he died young. And Petrarch, and Don Quixote."

"Interesting theories you have."

"I say the whole world thinks of nothing but love, and between the world and what isn't love, all that's left is a few gestures."

"I don't know," Diego said, "you'll end up convincing me."

"Nathalie thinks of nothing but love too. For her, being known means being loved. That's what drives you crazy with jealousy. It's true, it solves the problem of fidelity for her, knowing she's making so many men happy. Public happiness and public disaster make it so easy to be simple. That's what the world should be for, instead of tearing you to bits. To help you stay faithful. Lustful thoughts are the best thing in the world . . ."

Diego was very pale. Claudia knew she wouldn't tear him from his night.

"Your face is haggard, all you can think about is Nathalie. You don't even see the sky."

"Yes, I see the sky, and it's grey. You know, behind the wheel of a car you can't help being a little absent."

"Nathalie is your absence. You don't see anything any more. You're just half a man, and the half that's left is the one that loves Nathalie."

"So you're nagging a ghost."

"I love a ghost, it's the same thing. I'm running after a shadow. When I loved you, you were a man. Now all I have left is the landscape and there's nothing to see. You're going too fast."

"There's no time," Diego said.

"You want to see your unhappiness up close."

"I'm going to show you Saint-Philibert all the same," Diego said.

"Saints bore me."

"This isn't a saint," Diego said. "It's an amaz-
ing church."

"Is there time?" Claudia asked.

"There's always that kind of time."

How much I love going into places with him,
she thought.

The little wooden Virgin fascinated Claudia.

"How sad she looks. Has she suffered as much
as I have? Which is worse? Seeing your son on
the cross or not being loved?"

Diego was holding Claudia's hand. They
looked like two children who were coming to
make a vow.

"Your church is pink," Claudia said, caressing
the enormous columns. "How beautiful it is. So
enormous, and so gay."

"If I had to define beauty," Diego said, "I
think Romanesque art is the first thing I'd think
of."

"I'd like to see every detail," Claudia said.
"I'd like you to explain every column to me, and

the nave, and all the capitals. I want you to tell
me everything about Saint-Philibert."

"Just look," Diego said, "that's enough."

"Nathalie looks like the brown Virgin!"
Claudia exclaimed.

"All women look like the Virgin. You do too."

Claudia caressed the stones, the wood, the
roses. So much love. *Mine is in pencil. I'll be
erased. If only I could get back into the stone,
under the earth.* "It's easy," she said aloud.

"What?" Diego demanded.

"Believing in such things. Places like this
could make me a mystic."

"I wish they would," Diego sighed.

"Kiss me," Claudia answered.

When they left Tournus, Claudia felt they
were married.

"Does Nathalie like Romanesque art?"

"Yes, of course. You can't help liking it."

"You know," Claudia said, "once Nathalie
and I took a little trip together."

"When was that?" Diego asked.

"When you had gone to cover those accidents. The Pirandello year."

"But she was acting every afternoon and night then."

"We went on a Tuesday. There was no performance."

"Where did you go?"

"To Le Havre. She wanted to go to Le Havre."

"What did you do?"

"We went to a bar. We ate oysters, drank white wine, and danced with the sailors. It was fun. They all recognized Nathalie. It drove them crazy. They thought we were Lesbians because we'd decided not to sleep with anybody."

"Afraid of catching something?"

"Maybe. No. I think Nathalie was still in love with you then."

Claudia had Le Havre in her eyes. It was a winter evening. It was cold, the sea was green. One beautiful white steamer glittered in the harbor.

"Then we walked on the docks near Faidherbe, each of us with a lot of stupid sailors. She was so beautiful with her big pale eyes and her long hair. It looked as if she was searching for something."

"For what?"

"I don't know. You, maybe. That night I felt as if she was searching for you."

"What do you mean?" Diego asked.

"She was searching for you at Le Havre. Even though she knew you were at Cassis or somewhere."

"I was in Marseilles, I think."

"You see, another port. You should have found each other. Were you with another woman?"

"I don't think so," Diego said.

"Think hard."

"All right, I slept with Jeanne Villon in Marseilles."

"Well, you see, Nathalie felt it. In Le Havre she was miserable over you."

"How do you know?"

"She told me so. We slept in a little hotel that was called Front de Mer, or Marée, I don't remember. It was the first time I slept with her. I said: 'How beautiful you are,' and she laughed. I didn't exactly desire her, but she staggered me. I would have liked her to be a man at that moment, so that she could make love to me. It wasn't anything latent, it was just love. I don't know how to describe it, but we slept."

"Did she kiss you?"

"Yes, gently, like a little sister. I was afraid that touching me might disgust her, but I saw she was glad I was there. She said: 'Good night, little girl. Sometimes I need you, I love you,' and I stared at her and said: 'Diego's lucky.' And she answered: 'I'm lucky too, in a way, Claudia. I'm lucky, but life is complicated.' At that moment you were sleeping with Jeanne Villon."

"Maybe."

"She must have sensed it. Nathalie has her pythoness side. She usually sleeps until noon, but when I woke up that morning I saw her looking at the harbor. That's when she told me she had been in Le Havre with you."

Diego shuddered and grew a little paler.

"I even understood," Claudia continued, "why she wanted to go back there."

"Then what did she say?"

"That it was difficult to fit love, life, and work together. She cried when she said that. She told me not to tell you that we had been in Le Havre. Didn't she ever tell you, after?"

"No, never."

"I was glad to have a secret with her, even if at the start it was your secret."

"When did you leave?"

"Around one. We had lunch at Honfleur. We almost made ourselves sick on mussels. We were happy all over again. We got back to Paris in time for her play. I told her: 'You're boring in the Pirandello.' She said: 'You don't know how right you are. When I'm doing Pirandello I never know where I am.' "

For some time now they had been driving along the Saône. Claudia could think of nothing but the sea. She loathed these rivers that weren't the sea.

"You see," Claudia said, "I was talking about

Nathalie and you didn't even see Mâcon."

"But I know Mâcon."

"You know Nathalie, too."

"I don't think I do. And I don't know Jeanne Villon, or you, either. No one knows a woman. You're all little bundles of lies and contradictions."

"You pass through us like cities, without seeing us. Men know nothing about women. Women are really cruel. After a breakup, it's harder for a woman, but she forgets easier. We have a night memory: it fades quickly. Men have a real memory, though. Take you—you can't forget Nathalie."

"Not with you around, that's for sure," Diego said.

"Besides," Claudia continued, "you haven't the slightest idea what women's cynicism is like."

"Yes," Diego answered politely, "I can imagine very well."

"Besides," Claudia said, "we're like men in one thing, we have sudden bursts of abstract desire. There should be brothels for women. Sometimes I'd be glad to pay to make love with some-

one anonymous, just so as not to think about it
any more. You know, when the spring comes and
you feel a little depressed . . ."

"Yes," Diego said, "that would be really perfect for you: a brothel."

"Because we're like you, even if we prefer
having lovers who know our bodies, we sometimes want to have a boy, just like that, all of a
sudden. There, you see that tall blond boy by
the road there, that hitchhiking ephebe—I
wouldn't mind having him."

Diego slowed down.

"What are you doing?"

"I'm going to ask him where he's going."

"Are you crazy?"

Diego stopped the car. The tall blond boy
walked over.

"Marseilles?"

"Yes," Diego said. "Get in."

"Imbecile!" Claudia groaned.

"Salut," the ephebe answered.

"*English?*" Diego asked.

"*Nicht, Deutsch,*" the ephebe answered.

"He smells good," Claudia said.

"*Bitte*," the ephebe said. And he dozed off, after looking at his map.

Claudia, wild with fury, waked him up again.

"*Hamburg, ich bin Hamburg, sehr schön.*"

"*Yayaya.*"

"*Wi is her? woher kommen sie?*"

"Nuremburg."

"You see, he's an executioner's son."

"*Wo gehen sie?*"

"Paris, Marseilles, Genoa, Naples, Palermo, Bizerte, Algiers, Tangier, Cadiz, Madrid, Paris, Brussels, Hanover."

"And you never look at the countryside?" Claudia asked.

"*Yaya,*" the ephebe answered. And he dozed off again after looking once more at his map.

"You'll have to keep him a long time before he gets his strength back," Diego said. "Do you still like him?"

"Instead of putting on your jealous act, it would be better if you got rid of him."

"Why? He's nice."

"No, he's ridiculous."

"A minute ago you wanted to sleep with him."

"Just like that, doing seventy, abstractly. But not when it spoils the few hours we have together."

"He's not bothering us much."

"He's bothering me."

They reached a five-branched intersection. Diego slowed down.

The ephebe woke up abruptly:

"Wo bin ich?"

It was true, he never looked at the landscape and was interested only in the map he kept checking off with a red ball-point pen. Despite the jolting of the car, he *x*'d out each town he had passed through as he slept.

"His France is a real cemetery," Claudia said.

"Yaya." The ephebe smiled.

"France sehr schön?" she asked, when they saw the first sunflowers.

Then she smiled at him.

"Frauen französich sehr schön?"

"Ya ya," the ephebe answered a little anxiously, watching Diego.

Claudia smiled at him again. The ephebe lowered his eyes, like a girl.

"*Ihr name?*"

"Hermann."

"*Ich* Claudia."

"*Ihr mann?*"

"*Nicht mann, brüder.*"

The ephebe stared at them, disconcerted.

"Why did you tell him I was your brother?"

"You'll see."

Claudia began caressing Diego.

"Stop that, Claudia. I can't drive and you make me sick."

The ephebe stared wide-eyed.

"We have to make him believe that Frenchmen sleep with their sisters. Then he'll go back home with some new ideas. He'll never learn anything just staring at his map all the time."

"No doubt," Diego sighed.

She kissed him on the neck. The ephebe was writhing on the back seat. As she caressed Diego she kept glancing back at him. He was huddled in a corner.

"*Ich sehr schön?*" she asked him.

"Yaya," he murmured.

"Ich et tu?" Claudia asked. And she made an unmistakable gesture.

"I'll let you off here," Diego said. "It'll be perfect, right here in the fields."

The ephebe stared at them, dumbfounded. Claudia turned around and began caressing the tanned knee that emerged from his khaki shorts. He shrank a little farther away.

"Of course, he might be a homosexual."

"Each time you scare a man off, you think he's a homosexual."

"No, with you I'm used to it, but men adore each other in Germany, everyone knows that."

Claudia flashed another tender smile. The ephebe, scarlet now, struggled to answer, but managed only a grimace. Claudia ran her tongue over her lips. Hermann looked toward the car door. He was obviously regretting his dusty road.

"How stupid he looks."

"A minute ago you said he was handsome."

"Maybe at a distance, but he has no expression."

Diego looked at him through the rear-view mirror.

"It's true, he seems a little haggard."

"I'm going to frighten him as much as I can," Claudia said.

"We're going to have to stop for gas anyway."

He slowed down beside two red pumps and got out of the car. Claudia got out too and climbed in the back seat, beside the ephebe. She took his hand, which he pulled away. Suddenly she opened the door and began screaming as if the wretched Hermann were trying to rape her. The ephebe, terrorized, grabbed his knapsack and began running through the fields.

"What did you do to him?" Diego asked.

"I took his hand and he ran away. Men are such cowards. Imagine being scared of a woman like me."

"Yes, imagine," Diego said.

The girl who came out to give gas was pretty, plump and fresh. She smelled of the South, and poured out the gasoline as if it were wine.

"Your car was thirsty."

"Yes," Diego said, "I guess so."

"What's the matter with your friend?"

"He's a hitchhiker," Claudia said. "He thought I wanted to rape him. He got scared."

The young woman smiled.

"They're not very adventurous, these young people . . ."

Diego took out his wallet and paid.

"That's fine, Madame, thank you."

They got back into the car and rolled down all the windows.

"At least it gave us something to laugh at," Claudia said.

"Yes, but I'm afraid he'll make the rest of his trip on foot—at least as far as Marseilles."

"That'll be good for him. At least he'll look at the landscape."

The grass was strewn with orange tents pointed like steeples. They had passed Villefranche-du-Lyonnais.

The Aronde was driving through silkworm country. Claudia's laughter tore her to pieces.

She had been distracted from him. She felt panic-stricken. She had laughed just before dying. Why laugh? Diego, Diego, how she loved him.

Lyons was approaching like a guillotine.

I'll be beheaded in the Place Belcourt, she thought. A fine grey rain was gently executing her. *I won't even have seen the willows and the wistaria.*

The dreadful little church of Anse defied them with every one of its lozenges. They drove past acres of vines and bluish cabbages.

"In France," Claudia said, "everything I really love is south of Lyons."

"I like it even farther south, where it smells of sun, heather, *vin rosé*, bead curtains, and locusts, where people sing when they talk and aren't ever in a hurry."

If only we'd have engine trouble in Avignon for three days, or a bad blowout in Aix, Claudia dreamed.

Lyons, city of the heavyweight champion.
Lyons, city of silk.

Lyons, city that kills, Claudia read.

"I wish I could see the plane trees."

There had already been some, skimpy and pointed—false plane trees—but she had pretended not to see them.

Diego looked at the poplars growing alongside the road.

"If you knew how much I love plane trees."

"You'll see some," Diego said.

"The real plane trees are much farther south. You have to go a long way to see real plane trees."

"They begin a good ways before Lyons."

"No, they don't!" Claudia exclaimed. "You know nothing ever really begins before Lyons. Lyons has silk and quenelles and nothing else. I want to see plane trees."

"Plane trees," Diego answered, "grow on the Boulevard Saint-Michel and the Quai de Bercy, and there are more all along the road."

"No, I want to see real plane trees, Diego, not this kind. Wild ones that twist and curl, plane trees that make shade for people who only want the sun, the big plane trees of Provence and the sea, plane trees buried under locusts, not the plane trees with their little white shields that you see along the road."

The plane trees of Lyons surrounded her like judges.

"I want to see the plane trees of innocence."

"You think they exist?"

"I *know* they exist. Please. Don't abandon me before the plane trees, the real ones. Don't leave me until we get to a plane tree. Have pity on me, Diego, have pity on me!"

Claudia was crying and the city was there. Opaque, cruel. She closed her eyes when they passed through the tunnel. Claudia loved cities, yet all their horror sprang at her throat. She had forgotten the streetcars, the red lights, the drugstores, the rhythm of cities. They penetrated Lyons, Rue de la Claire, Rue de la Poste, Rue de Bourgogne. Her eyes full of tears, Claudia couldn't read any more.

DEATH TO THE REDS, shrieked the grey walls.

"I'm going to fall straight down into the Rhône," she said.

"No, you're not," Diego said, "it's always less terrible than you think."

They were approaching the station. It was raining.

"Diego, have pity on me. I want to leave you in the sun."

Diego didn't answer. He stopped the car in front of the word "Departures." She no longer saw anything clearly. He looked at her sadly, and took her arm.

"What time is the train for Paris, Madame?"

"The next one is at six forty-eight."

"There are none before that?"

"No, Monsieur."

Claudia was gradually getting used to her misery.

"Will you stay with me until the train leaves?"

"Two hours is a long time. I won't get to Valence until after dark."

"And to think that I may have another sixty years to live."

The station was enormous, grey, cruel.

There was no place to hide. Tickets were being punched. The station echoed to every despair. From behind their plastic sieves, the ticket sellers handed you your death sentence. Four thousand one hundred twenty francs. For that price, you're torn from the man you love. For nothing. For nothing. Nathalie doesn't love him any more. He doesn't love me. I'd like to jump in front of a train. Why didn't we get ourselves killed in the car? Diego and I. How I love him. Diego, Diego.

Nathalie, majestic in stations, walked like a queen. You're always cold in a railroad station. Without flowers, with flowers, you're always cold. Their little baggage carts are going to run over my toes. Claudia hated stations. They were always the end of something. The clock and its enormous hands tore apart her heart. Lyons, lion of the dead. Dying. Dying. I'm dying of love. Diego, I beg you. Not here. Not here.

"All right, come on," Diego said, "we'll go look for your plane trees."

The other half of Lyons rolled past like a poem. The streetcar rails looked like violin strings. Claudia turned on the radio. In front of them, as they were leaving Lyons, another hitch-hiker held out his thumb.

"Do you like this one?" Diego asked.

"No, he's hideous," and Claudia put her foot on top of Diego's, making the accelerator touch the floor.

A *paso doble* celebrated their wedding.

All the fatigue, all the anguish in the world had left her. She was stiff, though, as she was after making love, and calm.

"How good it is here," she said.

"Yes, it's good."

The locusts were making a deafening racket.

Here was Vienne. They had miraculously entered the South. France cut herself in two, like an apple. The North had fallen. They were among blue vines now, and locusts, and plane trees.

"Did you like traveling with Nathalie?" Claudia asked.

"Yes, a lot."

"Did you like the same things?"

"No, not at all, that's why we traveled well together. She taught me nights, and I taught her mornings. She liked people, I liked stones, I was always thirsty, she was always hungry."

"That's love."

"I don't know about that," Diego said, "but all the cities I've seen with her I know well."

"And the country?"

"The country too."

"What *didn't* you do well with Nathalie?"

"If you keep on asking, you might end up by finding out."

"We're buried under the locusts," Claudia said, "and a few minutes ago we were back in Lyons and it was raining."

"It's going to be beautiful in a few minutes, you'll see," Diego said.

"I'm happy."

"It's good here," Diego answered.

"Will you sleep with me tonight?"

"Listen, all we discussed was the plane trees. You said: 'I want to see the plane trees.' "

"But the plane trees are love. I told you I wanted to see plane trees, but I meant: 'I want to sleep with you.' "

"Oh," Diego said.

"I'm simple, aren't I?"

"Very simple."

"Is five hundred and seventy-two kilometers and two nights too much to ask?"

"I don't know," Diego said. "As soon as something exists, you destroy it with words."

"What do I destroy? What exists? Nothing. *Nothing.* You're driving toward Nathalie."

"Forget about us, Claudia, forget about us. Can't you forget us for a second?"

"No, never. You see, you still say 'us' when you mention her. And if I forget Nathalie, I remember I'm going to leave you."

"Look at the road for a while. How beautiful it is here. You can feel we're going toward the sun."

"I'll leave you before the sun, and the night will fall, and there won't be anything. I want to see plane trees. I want to see olive trees. I want to see the sea."

Methylene-blue wistaria was hanging along the walls. Bluer than Nathalie. Bluer than the sea. Bluer than blue. Worse. The wistaria of blue-jeans and bluing.

The road was covered with peaches. Claudia burst out laughing, nervously, without being able to stop.

"What's the matter with you?" Diego asked.

"Nothing, I'm just laughing. I'm laughing at my misery. If I cried I'd be screaming."

"You have a funny laugh," Diego said.

"Did you just notice it?"

"No, I just said you have a funny way of laughing."

"It's Nathalie's laugh, I'm imitating Nathalie laughing."

"That's right," Diego said. "I should have thought of it."

"I laugh the way she does, that's all. I've imitated her laugh to please you. Once I even imitated the way she makes love, to seduce you."

Plane trees slender as pretty girls bordered the road. Diego turned red.

"What do you mean?"

"I slept with someone who had slept with Nathalie. He told me something about her, at night, and I wanted to imitate her."

"Someone—who? What thing? What a bitch you are!"

"No, I'm not. I loved you, you didn't love me. I had to find something. And I could only get you with Nathalie's weapons."

"What man, what thing—bitch, you're all bitches!"

"There's nothing bitchy about loving."

"Shut up, I'm disgusted with you. If a man knew what was inside a woman's head and heart, he wouldn't get near her."

"In the head and everywhere else, we're superior."

"Don't start your theories again, you bore me stiff."

"I'm teaching you about women, aren't I?"

"You're teaching me about bitchery. You're all false, infamous, lying bitches!"

"We're not infamous, we're infinite."

"Most of all you're a pain in the ass."

At Livron, there were plane trees, plastic whips, and bars full of accordion music. Some signs mentioned nougat, but the South, the real South, pimento red, was here.

Acacias. Poplars. Cypresses. Sun.

Marseilles, Côte d'Azur.
Hôtel du Poisson-rouge.
Let the white bark of the plane trees be our real wedding, Claudia prayed.

They swam in plane trees. They were everywhere. Claudia knew it. She saw them. She was dizzy over them. She lost herself in plane trees. They passed at high speed, like a big set of ninepins. She counted, lost count, forgot. She squeezed herself against Diego.

"Cold?"

"No, I'm in the plane trees."

Basketwork of all colors sprouted along the road too. Driving through a village, they saw a fat woman coming through a bead curtain, then green tables set in the shade of the plane trees like four-leaf clovers, and men in blue on benches. After the village, fields of sunflowers, earth-suns turned toward the sky. They were in *vin rosé* and locust country.

"Shall we stop for a glass?"

"Yes," Diego said, "only near a garage."

"How relaxed you are, it's wonderful."

They discovered a garage where they could drink.

"Can you change the oil and do a grease job, Monsieur?" Diego asked.

"Of course," the man said. There were locusts in his throat, already.

"And do you have some *rosé* that's good and cold?"

"Of course."

The car was turning gold in the twilight. The road they had followed vanished into the night of time. Near Piolenc she was going to be happy.

"You see, I've run after you, but I've almost won. We've come to bead curtains, *vin rosé*, the voices that sing, even Provence. We can love each other tonight."

"Shut up."

"Listen, Diego, we've made love in hideous

furnished rooms, in filthy hotels, in cold beds, and now that we have the grass, the sea, and the crickets, you don't want me any more."

"Shut up."

Claudia stood up, sat down on the gravel, and put her head on Diego's knees. He pushed her away, gently.

"You know," she said, "I have to make up for a terrible thing."

"What?"

"After I broke up with Michel, I was still unsure of myself. I thought no one could ever desire me any more, and one day, in a bus, I picked up a man just to make sure, just to reassure myself that I was still a woman. It was near Saint-Jean-de-Luz. He told me: 'I'll drive you home in my car,' and near the sea, under a sky full of stars, we made love on the pine needles that smelled so good. The man was on top of me, heavy as the world, and the needles pricked me. I told myself—I was crying—'All this beauty and not Diego.'"

"So?"

"So I've never exorcised that beach."

"Was the man attractive?"

"No, he was strong."

"Very strong?"

"Yes, he didn't see the stars."

"But you saw them."

"That's all I saw, and then the headlights of cars—we weren't far from the road, at a turn—like the rays of the sun. It was upsetting."

"Did you ever sleep with him again?"

"No, never. He had too many stars attached to all his stupidity. And I want to exorcise that beach with you. Diego, listen to me. Make love to me on a beach."

"Who knows what we'll do?"

"You know," Claudia said, "I know it's over between us—but I want it to finish beautifully. I want one more night, just one. Tonight on a beach, with stars."

"But it's raining."

"That doesn't matter. We need a beach for the two of us, something big, something we can't ever forget."

"I won't forget you."

"But something as strong in your memory as

Nathalie, as strong as plane trees, as strong as locusts. Kiss me."

"Come on. The car's ready. Let's get going."

Diego stood up quickly, and Claudia followed him.

"Good-by, lovebirds," the garage man said.

They drove away. Claudia was wound around Diego like seaweed.

"We're going to drive all the way to the sea."

Diego didn't answer. The plane trees along the road looked like little leopards about to spring.

"I feel that you love me and that you're going to abandon me."

"I need to be alone."

"You want to purify yourself before meeting her again. But I won't taint you."

"That's not the question."

"It's as if you're always afraid I'll dirty something."

"Who told you that?"

"I'm telling myself that. I know I'm right. I beg you, Diego, let our story finish at the sea."

"We're a long way from the sea."

"We're so close to love. Look, Diego, all I can

see is plane trees and sunflowers. I want to roll in sunflowers."

"It's raining."

"That doesn't matter, I'll be close to you. You'll be my sunflower lover in the rain."

The sky was turning pink and blue. It was lowering over them. Night was falling, like a silk dyed darker. Claudia felt herself engulfed by love.

"Listen, just one night. Sunflowers, olive trees, and the sea. We'll have dinner in a little harbor. We'll eat melon, and drink *rosé*, we'll eat a fish that smells of grass, and you'll desire me. We'll prepare our last night like a wedding."

"What'll we eat for dessert?" Diego asked.

"We'll have melon again. We have to be crazy. And raspberries, and more wine, and then we'll go out onto the beach, we'll take off all our clothes, and you'll make love to me, and then we'll go into the sea."

"How will we dry off?"

"We'll roll on the sand. And then we'll make love again, and swim, and afterwards, when we

don't desire each other any more, we could run
on the beach until we're dry."

"Pretty tiring, for a fairy tale."

"If you'd rather not go in the water, we can
leave the sand on our bodies, but I think the sea
will be wonderful."

"You're not afraid of the jellyfish?"

"No, and not of your memory either. Tonight
is for us."

Claudia yielded to the darkness, surrounded
by the fields she loved. She dismissed Nathalie.
Nathalie-les-Avignon. Nathalie-of-the-truth and
Nathalie-of-the-lie.

She had left for the festival. It was there, without Diego, without Claudia, in her cardboard and
stone glory, that she had met the new man.

Avignon. Nathalie-of-all-the-Avignons. Claudia
was old with the memory of Diego. It was at
Avignon, in the center of the arena, that he had
lost her.

"What are you thinking about?" Diego asked.

The vines bathed in the red fields. The odors were there, and the smile of Orange. Huge plane trees were twined together, like their hearts.

"When did you see her the first time?"

"I didn't know you yet. She was in Chekhov's *Three Sisters*. I was wild about her voice. I went five times."

"And after?"

"After, one day, I found out her telephone number and I called her. When I heard her voice, I got scared and hung up. Another day, you answered. A man with Nathalie—I was scandalized. I hung up that day too."

"Your passion was beginning to be expensive."

"Then I telephoned again, and I said the Villons had told me to call. My voice trembled. Nathalie told me to come see her after the performance. When I went into her dressing room, you were there in a corner, smoking. She was very nice, but I don't remember any more how she let me into your lives—so gently, so kindly. I saw she wasn't afraid of me, and she was right. You paid no attention to me, nor I to you; it was only long afterward that I began to love you."

"Did she talk to you a lot?"

"Yes, about everything. I would have died for her voice. She told me: 'Little girl, you don't know anything about life, but if you concentrate, you'll make something of yourself.' She was right, I was going off in all directions at once."

"And then?"

"I still couldn't concentrate. I was afraid of being myself, and of no longer being Nathalie's object. I decided: 'If I become someone, I'll lose her. I prefer love.' "

"You were crazy."

"Yes, of course I was, but loving Nathalie meant more to me than anything else in the world, and then one night—it's so silly, I stood everything from Nathalie (the way you did), her rages, her whims, her teasing—the night of the opening of *Don Juan*, remember? I was sitting beside you, Nathalie came on more beautiful than ever, and when she began talking, beautiful as she was, I realized that she was 'acting'—not acting a part, just 'acting.' I saw it perfectly clearly, violently, and I also saw that you saw it, and that we couldn't tell her. There was a little voice talking inside my head, I listened to it, and I knew just how Nathalie should have been acting her part. It was the first day I could detach myself from her a little."

"I remember how badly she acted then. I didn't know you had noticed it."

"No one mentioned it in the papers. No one noticed it, except the two of us who loved her."

"How did you know I had noticed it?"

"Because I was watching you a lot too."

Nathalie, in her green velvet dress embroidered with pearls, appeared to both of them through the plane trees.

"What did she tell you when you talked together for hours?"

"She talked about everything—about her father, her childhood, her first husband, the early days when she was so poor, the war."

"And then?"

"She talked about you, too."

"And what did she say?"

"She made me fall in love with you."

"How?"

"By details. I couldn't tell you which ones now, but by tremendous details—your moral purity, your sense of poverty."

"I've never had a sense of poverty," Diego said. "I was poor, that's all."

"And she told me about your jealousy, too."

"It was Nathalie who was jealous."

"She told me you were jealous of her talent, of her success, of everything that took her away from you."

"No doubt. She was gradually losing her truth. She no longer had a sense of things."

"Once you wept when you saw her dressing room full of flowers."

"Did she tell you *why* I wept?"

"No, she just said tears ran down your face.

And once you took a bracelet off her wrist and stamped on it."

"What a fascinating vision of me you had! I was nothing but a clown in her stories."

"Still, I fell in love with you."

"No, Claudia, you don't 'fall in love.' Love isn't a fall. Anyway, the man you think you love is Nathalie's clown."

"But you *are* Nathalie's clown. You're going to try and find her. You can't do without her. She knows it, and she can do without you."

"Did she tell you so?"

"Yes, one night—I was already in love with you—she told me: 'Claudia darling, I once loved Diego more than anything in the world, but now I realize that I've stopped loving him.' She told me that the night of Paulo's birthday, when you were drunk and flirting with Jeanne Villon, and I hated you."

"What a bitch!"

"Why was she a bitch?"

"Because I thought that day was a day of truth between us."

"Well, it was a day of lies."

"She wanted to keep two men. I don't go halves."

"Once you had three women, Nathalie told me."

"That was true, but we weren't really in love with each other then."

"She never forgave you for it. And it all starts there. Nathalie left you because of your past. Because of your old lies. Maybe she doesn't love you any more now. You see," Claudia said, "for me the two of us are really through."

"I couldn't care less," Diego said, "but we're having a disgusting conversation, you and I. Ten years ago, I'd have died before talking like this."

"It's because of your prejudices that you lost Nathalie. She's stubborn, proud, even nasty, but she doesn't have any prejudices. She's freer than you are, and you thought you could teach her freedom."

"You don't know what you're talking about."

"Yes, I do, I know very well. When women have understood certain things . . ."

"They sleep with everyone. I know your theories."

"No, but they're capable of renunciation, and Nathalie has renounced you."

"I didn't want her to," Diego said.

"You didn't want her to, but you asked for it. It was your fault."

"You don't understand anything."

"No, I'm confused. I'm confused from loving you, and I'm losing everything, but I don't care now. Nathalie's lost for you too, and you lost me before you ever had me because you're afraid of women, afraid of their truth. Yes," Claudia continued, "it's from fear of women, from love of women, that you lost Nathalie. You loved Nathalie badly and you didn't let her love you. That's why you lost her. What women want is to love. Being loved always disgusts us a little."

"Really?"

"Yes, really. We want to love. Nathalie is more than loved, and you loved her badly. She wanted to love someone who would let himself be loved. That's what she's found with Simon! And I can't love you either—I'm going too."

"*Au revoir.*"

"You see, you love Nathalie and you've lost her by love."

"Are we still a long way from the sea?" Claudia asked.

"Yes," Diego said, "and I can't spend the night with you."

"Why? One night? What's one night?"

"I can't."

"Just one night, Diego," Claudia said mechanically, "the last night. I swear it. Listen, even if you want to, we won't go to the sea. We'll stop at Avignon, just after the ramparts, you'll take me into a hotel room, you'll stay with me, and at dawn you'll go away all alone. I'll take the train then. I swear I will."

"Don't make it worse," Diego said. "Leave me alone."

"Don't send me away, Diego, please!" Claudia cried, pursuing her litanies. "The road is covered with sunflowers."

The little arch of Orange was there, like a poem in the middle of the square.

He's killing me, drowning me. He's deaf, or he couldn't help hearing so much love.

"This beach—you used to love it."

"I can't, Claudia, don't insist."

"Try, please, Diego."

"I can't."

"Then let's have a last drink together."

"If you want to."

They drove into Avignon. The men looked like mosquitoes along the ramparts. They were lit by spotlights.

How ridiculous unhappiness is, how tiny, Claudia thought, *but how I love him!*

They parked in front of a little bar.

"What time is the train to Paris, Madame?"

"Ten fifty-five, Monsieur."

"You see, we still have an hour."

"I hate you."

"Listen," Diego said, "don't try to fight me

any more. I'm not your enemy. Even last night was too much. I don't regret it, but don't make things bad now."

"No, I don't want anything any more."

"That's better."

"You know, you can discourage even the best will in the world. We'll have had sixty-one hours of happiness. That's not so bad."

"Probably," Diego said, "and it's not over."

Claudia was drinking *vin rosé* in little sips, as if it were a drug.

"It is for me. I suffer too much."

"What do you mean?"

"It's out of proportion. Whatever happiness we have, I make for us. I think too much about you, and when I stop being with you I'm all deteriorated inside—inhuman, stupefied."

"That's what love is like."

"Maybe, but since you won't accept it, I think it's better to nip it in the bud."

"I don't know," Diego said. "I don't know myself."

"You love Nathalie. I understand you, I love her too. I see there's no room for me. So we'll stop with this blue road, these six hundred ninety-seven kilometers, these plane trees, and this *vin rosé*. We'll stop before the melon and the sea."

"You're beautiful when you're energetic like this."

"I'm always energetic, but you don't like my strength except when it takes me away from you."

"Sometimes it seems to me you know me very well."

"Yes," Claudia said, "I think so."

"Maybe you love me better than anyone ever has."

"Maybe, I don't know."

"I'm unhappy, you know that."

"Yes, but everyone's unhappy. Listen," Claudia said, "I don't want to lose myself in you any more. It hurts me too much. You're right. We'll leave each other."

"Wait a minute," Diego said, putting his hand on Claudia's. She pulled away.

"No, once I'm with you, I lose myself again. You can only lose yourself if there's an echo. With you there's no echo. I have to go."

"Listen, Claudia, don't be so sudden."

"I'm listening, but I don't hear you any more. I love you, but I don't have the strength to go on any more."

"I can't sleep with you tonight," Diego said.

"I didn't ask you to. I'm the one who wanted to sleep with you. I'm the one who wanted to have you. You can't have me any more because I've resigned myself. You see, with you I'm already far away. No, I wanted not-to-have you one more time, but it's over."

"Claudia, what kind of act are you putting on?"

"I'm pretending to try not to love you any more. Women can do anything."

"Don't start that again."

"Yes," Claudia said, "we're born for lying. So when we tell the truth, there's a terrible upset. Here we are with our femininity *and* our truth; it doesn't work. I'm not lying to you. I'm not acting a love scene. I'm acting a farewell scene. The train is at five to eleven. Come on. I want to get used to leaving you."

Diego followed her. People didn't understand this couple that obviously desired each other and were separating. Claudia got into the Aronde, put her high-heeled shoes back on, and tossed the red espadrilles out on the road.

"What are you doing?"

The espadrilles looked like faded poppies in the darkness. Claudia wanted to scream.

"I don't want you to give them to Nathalie."

Diego was tense, sad.

"Kiss me," Claudia said.

The railroad platform was deserted. They began trembling.

"Go away!" she screamed.

She watched Diego walk away. He looked old. *If he turns around, I'll die.*

When she opened her eyes again, it was dawn in Paris. It was the first time she had come out of a station empty-handed. She was walking very fast on her little heels.

I look like a whore who couldn't find any customers in Avignon, she thought.